Gabriel Harrower Parkhurst

John Parkhurst

Gabriel Harrower Parkhurst

John Parkhurst

ISBN/EAN: 9783337396466

Printed in Europe, USA, Canada, Australia, Japan

Cover: Foto ©Raphael Reischuk / pixelio.de

More available books at **www.hansebooks.com**

JOHN PARKHURST,

BORN MAY 2, 1760, AT WESTON, MASSACHUSETTS,

HIS ANCESTORS AND DESCENDANTS.

PREPARED BY

GABRIEL H. PARKHURST,

BATH, NEW YORK.

1897.

To Lillian,

now in Heaven, I dedicate this little

volume which she helped to make.

ONE of the pleasantest returns to the writer for his labor in compiling this little work has been the many courtesies he has received from his kinsmen and friends all over the world, who have generously aided in making this record what it is. To them, one and all, he offers sincere thanks. But he feels especially indebted to the following for the assistance they have freely and frequently given:

CAPT. CHARLES D. PARKHURST, of Fortress Monroe, Va.

MR. WALTER CUSHING PARKHURST, of Baltimore, Md.

MR. EDSON SALISBURY JONES, of Port Chester, N. Y.

DR. LEWIS EVANS PARKHURST, M. A., of London, Eng.

REV. WILLIAM H. PARKHURST, of Cape Colony, S. Africa.

English · Family.

THE word "Parkhurst" is of Norman and French derivation, being composed of "parc" (French for park) and "hurst" (the Anglo-Saxon for wood). The family name dates back to the entrance of William the Conqueror in England, and the derivation of the word suggests that it was contemporaneous with the beginning of French influence in England. The word "Parkhurst" first appears in the Doomsday book, published in 1086, which mentions "Parkhurst forest" in the Isle of Wight. This was the earliest recorded royal park, a district of three thousand acres, nominally held by the government. It was, however, a public common, and was enclosed in 1815, eleven hundred and fifty acres being reserved by the crown as a nursery for navy timber. Near this is a village called Parkhurst, and a few miles away is Osborne House, Queen Victoria's winter residence. [Murray's Handbook of Surrey, Hants and the Isle of Wight, (1876) page 427.]

The family emigrated from the Isle of Wight between four and five hundred years ago, and built "Parkhurst Manor," in Surrey County, England, between Epsom and Guilford. Here is where we find the earliest authentic record of the family, in George Parkhurst, of Guilford, who was the father of Bishop John Parkhurst, born at Guilford, Surrey County, in 1511. George Parkhurst was living at Guilford the latter part of the XVth century. George Parkhurst, Jr., of Watertown, Mass., named his oldest son John, and this custom has been continued by his descendants, including the present generation. Dr. Lewis E. Parkhurst, of London, who belongs to the Guilford (Surrey County) branch, states that there has been a similar custom of naming the eldest son John in his family, in England, for many generations.

Parkhurst Manor, about twenty-five miles south of London, between Epsom and Guilford, remained in possession of the family until 1745. In 1629, Sir Robert Parkhurst, who was afterward Lord Mayor of London, held his court there. From Surrey County the family seems to have divided into four branches, viz : Guilford, Norfolk, London and Catesby, whose coats-of-arms are identical, showing beyond question their common ancestry. From which one of these branches the American family sprang has not yet been conclusively proved, but in all probability George Parkhurst, of Guilford, Surrey County, was the great grand-father of George Parkhurst, who settled in Watertown, Mass. The name George appears almost exclusively in this branch, as well as the name John, which first comes into the family with Bishop John Parkhurst in 1511–1512. We find the same combination of family names in this branch, which exists in the American family, namely : George Parkhurst, naming his son George, and George Parkhurst, Jr., naming his son John. The names George and John appear very rarely, if at all, in the other branches of the English family.

Manning and Bray's History of Surrey, Vol. 1, shows the following Parkhursts living in Guilford :

George Parkhurst, Sr., 30 Henry VIII (1539).

George Parkhurst, Jr., 30 Henry VIII (1539), page 32.

George Parkhurst, Mayor of Guilford, 1522, 1529, 1536, page 38.

Henry Parkhurst, Mayor of Guilford, 1573, page 39.

Thomas Parkhurst, Mayor of Guilford, 1604, 1609, 1615, 1623, 1634, page 39.

George Parkhurst, father of Bishop John, page 79.

Bishop John Parkhurst was a " Bachelor of Divinitie " at Oxford in 1529. Three years later he entered holy orders, though more fond of poetry and oratory than divinity. At length he became rector of the rich church of Clive, in Gloucestershire, where he did much good by his hospitality and charity. Soon after the death of King Edward, on account of his liberal views he incurred the displeasure of Queen Mary, and was for a time in danger of his life. He went into exile at Zurich, Switzerland, during the remainder of her reign. Returning to England, he was appointed Bishop of Norwich by Queen Elizabeth in 1560, which he held until his death, February 2d, 1574. (Visitation of Norfolk, 1563, Norfolk Arch. Soc., Vol. 2, page 15.) He translated the "Apocrypha" in the Bible, commanded by Queen Elizabeth, and was the author of a number of Latin works, some of his unpublished manuscripts still remaining at the British Museum. His father's coat-of-arms was similar to that shown in the cut. The three crescents were added when John was elected bishop.

Another crest used by the Guilford (Surrey) and the Norfolk branches is a silver buck's head erased out of a palisado coronet of gold. For illustrations see Fairbank's crests, plates 128, No. 21; 66, No. 2; 67, No. 13; 68, No. 2; 49, No. 4.

Among the famous Parkhursts of the XVIIIth century was the Rev. John Parkhurst, of Catesby, Northamptonshire, England, who was the author of the first Greek lexicon, which is still in use. He died in 1797, without issue, and was buried in Epsom church, where there is a monument to his memory. The churches and churchyards of Epsom, Abinger, Dorking and Guilford, are rich in memorials of dead members of the Parkhurst family.

American Family.

.

1   **George Parkhurst,** founder of the Parkhurst family in this country, emigrated from England about 1635. He brought at least two children with him (George, Jr., and Phebe), and is known to have been living in Watertown, Mass., in 1642. He was probably a man of considerable means, for he owned a large tract of land, besides a homestead of twelve acres. In 1643 he was admitted freeman. He married his second wife, Susanna, widow of John Simpson, in 1645, by whom he had no children. The same year he sold his Watertown estate and moved to Boston. (Bond's Hist. Watertown, Mass., pages 388, 391.)

Register N. E. Hist. and Genealogical Society, Vol. 27, page 364, states that George Parkhurst had the following children :

2   GEORGE, JR., born in England about 1618; married (1st) Sarah Browne, December 16th, 1643.

3   BENJAMIN, born in England.

4   JOSEPH, he moved to Chelmsford, Mass., but at what date is uncertain. He was, however, living there from 1656 to 1667. He married Mary Read, of. Chelmsford, at Concord, Mass., June 26th, 1656, and his name appears as one of the proprietors of the new field in Chelmsford. His share of twelve acres was allotted to him January 12th, 1666–7 (Allen's Hist. Chelmsford, page 169).

5   PHEBE, born in England ; married Thomas Arnold in 1640.

       THOMAS ARNOLD came to this country in May, 1635. He was admitted freeman in 1640. In October, 1651, he was fined twenty shillings by the court

for offense against the law concerning baptism.
April 2d, 1654, he was fined five pounds for neglecting public worship twenty days. April 2d, 1655,
he was fined ten pounds for neglecting public worship forty days, and his land was levied upon to pay
it (Bond's Hist. Watertown, Mass., page 9). He
seems to have inherited his sturdy independence
from his ancestors. Arnold was able to trace his
ancestry back through seventeen generations to
Ynir, King of Gwentland, A. D., 1100, who was a
direct descendant of Wessex, who was king of the
Britons from 688 to 728.

6   DEBORAH, married John Smith.

7   ELIZABETH, married (1st) Emanuel Hilliard ; (2d) Joseph
Merry.

8   MARY, married Rev. Thomas Carter.

2   **George Parkhurst, Jr.,** son of George Parkhurst (1),
the emigrant, was born in England in 1618 ; married (1st)
Sarah Browne, December 16th, 1643. She was the daughter
of Abraham and Lydia Browne, descendant of John Browne,
who was Mayor of Stamford, England, in 1376 and 1377.
He married (2d) Mary Pheza, September 24th, 1650. She
died March 9th, 1680–1, and he died March 16th, 1698–9,
aged 81 years. The old Parkhurst farm, where he probably
settled, was on the east side of Beaver brook and north side
of the County road, and the house stood a few rods east of the
new cottage of Mr. Thomas Page (" Watertown "). He had
two children by his first wife :

9   JOHN, born June 10th, 1644 ; married, about 1670, Abigail
Garfield.

10   SARAH, born September 14th, 1649, probably died young.

9   **John Parkhurst,** son of George Parkhurst, Jr. (2), and
Sarah Browne, born June 10th, 1644 , married, about 1670,
Abigail Garfield, daughter of Samuel and Susanna Garfield.

She was born June 29th, 1646, and died October 18th, 1726. He was admitted freeman April 18th, 1690. He died September 12th, 1725. They had nine children:

11   JOHN, born February 26th, 1671–2; married Abigail Morse.

12   ABIGAIL, born September 10th, 1674.

13   SARAH, born November 26th, 1676; married October 16th, 1700, Edward Sherman.

14   RACHEL, born December 30th, 1678; married, December, 1699, Abraham Gale.

15   ELIZABETH, born September 18th, 1681; married, December 31st, 1701, Joseph Ball.

16   MARY, born December 23d, 1683; married, May 1st, 1707, Edward Sanderson.

17   GEORGE, born January 3d, 1685–6; married, April 19th, 1726, Tabitha Fulham.

18   SAMUEL, born April 11th, 1688; married, May 27th, 1716, Sarah Shattuck.

19   HANNAH, born April 17th, 1690; married, January 3d, 1716, John Newton, of Marlborough, New Hampshire.

11   **Deacon John Parkhurst,** son of John Parkhurst (9) and Abigail Garfield, born February 26th, 1671–2; married Abigail Morse, a descendant of Joseph Morse, who came to this country in 1634, from England. She was born August 6th, 1677, and died May 3d, 175–. He settled in Watertown Farms, Weston, Mass. Was an original member, and one of the first deacons, of Weston church; elected January 4th, 1709–10. On January 21st, 1734–5, he gave to each of his sons, Isaac and Jonas, by deed of gift, eighty and one-half acres of land in Newton, Mass., bought from Caleb Gardner, then of Newport, Rhode Island. They had ten children:

20   JOHN, born and died 1695.

21   JOHN, born April 29th, 1697.

22   ABIGAIL, born June 20th, 1699; married, September 23d, 1728, John Pike, of Newbury.

23 LYDIA, born July 21st, 1701; married, April 11th, 1723, Joseph Stone, of Framingham, Mass.

24 ELIZABETH, born April 5th, 1704; died December, 1732, unmarried.

25 JOSIAH, born February 9th, 1706; married, October 23d, 1735, Sarah Carter.

26 ISAAC, born July 9th, 1708; married, February 7th, 1733-4, Lydia Bigelow.

27 MARY, born July 15th, 1710; married, August 20th, 1731, Edmund Bailey, of Newbury.

28 JONAS, born August 20th, 1712; married Abigail Bigelow, daughter of Joshua Bigelow and Hannah Fiske; date of marriage not found. Admitted to Congregational church in Milford by letter from Weston, 1747.

29 JEMIMA, born June 5th, 1715; married, April 20th, 1738, Benjamin Bartlett, of Newbury.

25 **Josiah Parkhurst,** son of Deacon John Parkhurst (11) and Abigail Morse, born February 9th, 1706, at Weston, Mass.; married, October 23d, 1735, Sarah Carter, daughter of Daniel and Sarah Carter, of Weston, Mass. She was baptized May 25th, 1728. They had six children:

30 JOSIAH, Jr., born March 8th, 1736-7; married, June 1st, 1758, Elizabeth Bigelow.

31 NATHAN, born November 2d, 1738; married (1st), February 9th, 1764, Elizabeth Shepard; (2) March 21st, 1765, Mary Ames, of Framingham. He, with his wife, Mary, and daughter, Elizabeth, moved to Framingham March 16th, 1769.

32 MARY, born March 3d, 1743; married, 1763, Samuel Fiske, of Weston. She died June 18th, 1773.

33 SARAH, born September 21st, 1747; married, April 15th, 1770, Isaac Flagg.

34 AMOS, born April 2d, 1756.

35 LYDIA, born May 10th, 1758.

30   **Josiah Parkhurst Jr.**, son of Josiah Parkhurst, Sr.
(25), and Sarah Carter, born March 8th, 1736–7, at Weston,
Mass. Married, June 1st, 1758, Elizabeth Bigelow, daughter
of Nathaniel Bigelow and Hannah Robison, of Newton. She
was born May 17th, 1738. He first settled in Weston, and
in 1762 removed to Framingham, building a house which he
located a few rods north of the railroad bridge, east of the
Concord river near the subsequent site of the " Cutler Mills."
The location was covered by the embankment of the Boston
and Worcester railroad in 1835. He was a member of the
Training Band in Weston, April 18th, 1757. This service
entitles his descendants to membership in the "Society of
Colonial Wars " (Mass. Archives, Vol. 95, page 277). At two
periods he lived in Marlborough N. H., where he died in
1832, in his ninety-fifth year. Their first three children were
born in Weston, and the other children in Framingham. They
had eleven children :

36   HANNAH, born March 27th, 1759; married February
25th, 1779, Jonathan Adams, and moved into Pennsylvania.

37   JOHN, born May 2d, 1760 ; married December 17th, 1783,
Sarah Bullard.

38   AARON, born June 1st, 1761 ; married, in Bellingham,
Sally Thompson, and removed to Stafford, Conn.

39   ELIZABETH, born in Framingham, February 28th, 1763 ;
married, May —, 1784, Samuel Walker.

40   EPHRAIM, born January 16th, 1765 ; married (1st), Decem-
ber 27th, 1788, Elizabeth Look. She died December 25th, 1825.
He subsequently married Mrs. Mary Adams, who died in 1870.
Ephraim died January 20th, 1850, at Framingham, Mass.
Many of his descendants are prominent in public life, among
them Dr. Charles H. Parkhurst, pastor of the Madison Square
Presbyterian church, the anti-Tammanyite reformer in New
York city.

41   LUCY, born June 19th, 1766; married, January 15th,
1794, Abraham Fisher ; died in 1845.

42   SARAH, born January 6th, 1768 ; married Micajah Morse,
and moved to New Hampshire ; died in 1814.

43 EUNICE, born November 20th, 1769; married ——— Becket, and lived in Unity, N. H.; died in 1829.

44 MOLLY, born November 15th, 1771; married, 1793, Josiah Hemenway, of Framingham.

45 LYDIA, born June 28th, 1775; married, August 19th, 1794, Solomon Becket, of Framingham.

46 JOSIAH, JR., born May 25th, 1778; married, April 2d, 1801, Nancy Jones, and moved to Marlborough, N. H.

John Parkhurst.

37   **John Parkhurst,** the son of Josiah Parkhurst, Jr. (30),
and Elizabeth Bigelow, was born May 2d, 1760, at Weston,
Mass.   In 1762 his father moved from Weston to Framingham, Mass., which was his home during the Revolution.   In
the summer of 1777, when seventeen years of age, he joined
the army.   His first service was to guard Continental stores
at East Sudbury.   On April 1st, 1778, he re-enlisted in Captain Holmes' company, Colonel Jonathan Reed's regiment,
being the first regiment of guards.   His first duty was to
guard British prisoners at Prospect Hill, Cambridge, who had
been captured with General Burgoyne.   He was discharged
July 4th, 1778, and at once re-enlisted for six weeks, in the
company commanded by Captain Amos Perry, of Sherburn.
He went with the company to Providence and Lewiston, R.
I., where his duty again consisted in guarding Continental
stores.   In August the company was engaged in building
redoubts near Newport, R. I.   July 24th, 1780, he enlisted
in Captain Walter McFarland's company, of Colonel Cyprian
Howe's regiment, Middlesex County regiment, for service in
Rhode Island.   The company went to Providence, guarding
stores on College Hill.   John Parkhurst was discharged
October 30th, 1780 (Mass. Arch., Vol. 35, page 124; Vol. 21,
page 111; Vol. 46, pages 13–14; Vol. 19, page 182).

This service entitles his descendants to membership in
the societies of the "Sons of the American Revolution" and
"Daughters of the American Revolution."

On December 17th, 1783, he married Sarah Bullard, who
died February 8th, 1818, at Springfield, Pa.   In 1813, John
Parkhurst, in company with William Evans, left New Hampshire to find a new home in the West.   They would have
settled in Monroe County, N. Y., but for the frontier troubles

then existing. Turning southward, they finally located in Springfield, Bradford County, Pa., where they built a comfortable log house. They returned to New Hampshire for their families, and in the fall of 1813, after a hard journey of six weeks, they arrived at the log house. Work was immediately commenced on a better house, and two years later (1815) the present homestead was completed. It was the home of John Parkhurst until his death, in 1836, and is still occupied by his descendants. The house is a substantial structure, commanding a beautiful view of Mount Pisgah and adjacent valleys.

He kept a diary for thirty years, wherein he states that he was only prevented from enlisting the fourth time by ill health. His diary shows that he took great interest in the militia while he lived in New Hampshire. During the later years of his life in Springfield he was invariably known by the title of "Major." He was elected to this office in the general training bands, which were annually organized in that vicinity. Mrs. Martha Bullock, who knew John Parkhurst in her childhood, still remembers seeing him with epaulettes on his shoulders, and a long black feather, tipped with red, in his hat.

Although a physician by profession, there is no record that he was ever in active practice. His life seems to have been occupied in farming, although he conducted a general store for some years at Marlborough, N. H. His diary reveals many characteristics of his sturdy life. Under date of July 20th, 1811, it contains the following excellent advice, upon the occasion of his paying $1,905.16 for having endorsed a friend's note: "So that it appears that I am this sum the poorer for dealing with one dishonest man, which I did merely to oblige him, without any promise, or even prospect, of reward, which I hope will be sufficient warning to all (my family, at least) never to be bound for any man without ample security; and again I say, not without ample security."

John Parkhurst was an active member of the church. He was a man of strong political views, and contributed to the

various periodicals of the time. In appearance he is remem-
bered as a distinguished-looking man, with keen blue eyes,
white hair, and a refined manner. He died November 1st,
1836, sitting in the rocking chair which he had brought with
him from New Hampshire, and was buried at Springfield. He
had nine children, all by his first wife, Sarah Bullard. The
first two were born in Framingham, the rest in Marlborough.
He married (2d), October 31st, 1822, Margaret Randel, of
Canton, Pa. The nine children were:

47   JOHN, JR., born December 30th, 1784; married, September 8th, 1822, Laura Gleason.

48   DANIEL, born May 6th, 1787; married, October 23d,
1817, Alma Allen.

49   JOSIAH, born March 12th, 1789; married, —— —, 1813,
Rachel Harkness.

50   SARAH MARIA, born April 10th, 1793; married, September 5th, 1813, William Evans.

51   CURTIS, born July 2d, 1794; married, November 11th,
1830, Jane Ann Kasson.

52   DEXTER, born September 21st, 1797; married, July 4th,
1823, Marian Speer.

53   JOEL, born April 8th, 1800; married (1st), November 16th,
1835, Emeline R. Allen; (2d) May 14th, 1856, Martha Harrower Steel.

54   MARTHA, born April 2d, 1803; married, July 25th,
1827, Micajah Seely.

55   EBENEZER F., born November 1st, 1807; married, November 8th, 1829, Dennis Brown.

47   **Dr. John Parkhurst, Jr.,** son of John Parkhurst
(37) and Sarah Bullard, was born December 30th, 1784, at
Framingham, Mass. He studied medicine with Dr. Carter,
of Keene, N. H., graduated at Dartmouth Medical College at
Hanover, and removed to Richmond, N. H., about 1810. He
was the author of the New England Diary and Almanac

for 1808 and 1809, a copy of which is in the possession of
Charles Tubbs, Esq., of Osceola, Pa.

On September 8th, 1822, he married Laura Gleason,
daughter of Windsor Gleason, Sr., and Sophia Clark, who
was born April 24th, 1797, at Langdon, N. H. He practiced
medicine until 1840, when on a visit to his brother in Springfield, Pa., he was taken sick, and died September 15th, 1840.
He was survived less than a year by his wife, who died at
Richmond, N. H., August 19th, 1841. They had three
children :

56   JOHN, JR., born February 13th, 1823; married (1st),
November, 1840, Lucy Buffum ;_(2d) September 14th, 1852,
Rebecca Kennedy.

57   ELIZABETH, born September 17th, 1820; married, October 1st, 1848, Dr. Leander Smith, of Beecher's Island, Pa.
She died December 28th, 1851.

58   JOEL G., born December 15th, 1828; married, April 28th,
1867, Grace L. Lyman.

---

56   **John Parkhurst, Jr.**, son of Dr. John Parkhurst, Jr.
(47), and Laura Gleason, born February 13th, 1823, at Richmond, N. H. ; married, November, 1840, Lucy Buffum. She
died in 1842, at Richmond. They had one child :

59   JOHN EDGAR, born August 14th, 1841 ; died at Alex-
ander, Va., May 22d, 1865. He was First Lieutenant in
Company H, 207th Pennsylvania Volunteers. " Parkhurst
Post," No. 35, G. A. R., of Elkland, Pa., was named after
him. The Post was reorganized in 1882, and took No. 581.

John Parkhurst, Jr., married (2d), September 14th, 1852,
Rebecca Kennedy, daughter of Luin P. Kennedy and Mary
A. Hulburt, born April 5th, 1828, at Arkport, N. Y. ; died
December 25th, 1893, at Binghamton, N. Y., and buried at
Elkland, Pa. He died January 20th, 1890. He came to
Elkland soon after his father's death and entered into active
business, first as a merchant, and later, for many years, as a

partner with his uncle, Joel Parkhurst, in the banking business, under the name of Joel Parkhurst & Co. After his uncle's death the name of the bank was changed, and he carried on the business with his son, Luin K. Parkhurst, and Charles L. Pattison, a son-in-law of Joel Parkhurst. The bank was considered one of the strongest financial institutions in that section of the state. It is now called the Pattison National Bank. He had three children by this marriage :

60   LUIN K., born June 1st, 1856; married, June 30th, 1881, Mary W. Reed.

61   CARRIE E., born August 5th, 1863; married, October 7th, 1886, William E. Williams.

62   JOHN WALTER, born August 9th, 1867 ; married, October 18th, 1888, Helen B. Moon.

---

60   **Luin K. Parkhurst,** son of John Parkhurst, Jr. (56), and Rebecca Kennedy, born June 1st, 1856, at Elkland, Pa. ; married, June 30th, 1881, Mary W. Reed, daughter of James M. and Albertine Reed, born December 22d, 1859, at Owego, N. Y. He was connected with his father and Charles L. Pattison in the banking business for several years at Elkland. He is now president of the First National Bank of Reed City, Mich., which is his home. They had three children :

63   FRANK A., born October 15th, 1883.

64   J. REED, born January 12th, 1887.

65   EDGAR, born October 13th, 1890.

---

61   **Carrie Elizabeth Williams,** daughter of John Parkhurst, Jr. (56), and Rebecca Kennedy, born August 5th, 1863, at Elkland, Pa. ; married, October 7th, 1886, William E. Williams, and resides at Reed City, Mich. They had three children :

66   JULIA R., born October 17th, 1887.

67   HELEN, born March 19th, 1888 ; died May 29th, 1895.

68   GLADYS E., born December 12th, 1892.

62 **John Walter Parkhurst,** son of John Parkhurst, Jr. (56), and Rebecca Kennedy, born August 9th, 1867, at Elkland, Pa.; married, October 18th, 1888, Helen Buel Moon, daughter of Rev. Solomon H. Moon and Charlotte Brandt. He left for Reed City, Mich., soon after his marriage, to engage in the banking business with his brother, occupying the position of cashier of the First National Bank of that city. They had two children:

69 JOHN, born December 7th, 1889; died July 31st, 1890.
70 GERTRUDE H., born September 19th, 1891.

---

58 **Joel G. Parkhurst,** son of Dr. John Parkhurst, Jr. (47), and Laura Gleason, born December 15th, 1828, at Richmond, N. H.; married, April 28th, 1867, Grace L. Lyman, daughter of Dr. Harry Lyman and Fanny DeCorseau, born October 15th, 1835, at Roulette, McKean County, Pa. She resides at Springwater, N. Y. He died August 15th, 1877, at Elkland, Pa. His business was that of a merchant and lumberman, in which he was actively engaged for twenty-five years. A genial, big-hearted man, with many friends. They had one child:

71 LEONA M., born January 29th, 1868; married, June 18th, 1884, Ernest W. Brown.

---

71 **Leona Maud Brown,** daughter of Joel G. Parkhurst (58) and Grace L. Lyman, born January 29th, 1868, at Elkland, Pa.; married, June 18th, 1884, Ernest W. Brown, a lawyer at Springwater, N. Y. They had one child:

72 ELNORA M., born April 11th, 1885.

---

48 **Dr. Daniel Parkhurst,** son of John Parkhurst (37) and Sarah Bullard, born May 6th, 1787, at Framingham, Mass. On October 23d, 1817, he married Alma Allen. He died at his father's home in Springfield, Pa., April 3d, 1819. They had no children.

49 **Josiah Parkhurst,** son of John Parkhurst (37) and Sarah Bullard, born March 12th, 1789, at Marlborough, N. H.; married, 1813, Rachel Harkness, daughter of John Harkness and Rachel McNall, born 1794, who came from Massachusetts to Springfield, Pa., in 1806. She died at Waukegan, Ill., October 31st, 1868. His first farm was near that of his father's, in Springfield, which he sold and moved to what was then called Addison Hill, near Elkland, Pa., where he lived until about 1860. He then left for the West. He died at Waukegan, Ill., April 1882, aged ninety-three years. They had eight children, all born at Springfield, Pa. :

73 NANCY, born 1815; married, August, 1871, Oliver Stephens. She died September 15th, 1887, at Toledo, O.

74 ELIZA AMES, born 1819; resides at Waukegan, Ill.

75 DANIEL DEXTER, born January 26th, 1821; married, November 21st, 1846, Sarah Lamb.

76 BEEBY BOYD, born February 8th, 1824; married, August 21st, 1848, Emeline Mack.

77 CORDELIA, born January 17th, 1827; married, November 2d, 1845, Horace Chandler.

78 HARRIET, born July 4th, 1830; married, November 2d, 1865, John Wells; resides in Toledo, O.

79 JOEL C., born 1833; died August 1st, 1865, at Elkland, Pa.

80 JANE, born 1835; died in 1843.

----

75 **Daniel Dexter Parkhurst,** son of Josiah Parkhurst (49) and Rachel Harkness, born January 26th, 1821, at Springfield, Pa.; married, November 21st, 1846, Sarah Lamb, of Troy, Pa. She died March 24th, 1894, at Toledo, O. He resides at Toledo, O. They had four children :

81 SAMUEL DEXTER, born December 7th, 1847; married, 1874, Ida M. Stratford.

82 CURTIS R., born August 26th, 1849; died September, 1850.

83 EDWARD H., born January 15th, 1854; resides in Chicago, Ill.

84 GRACE, born February 15th, 1858; resides in Toledo, O.

81 **Samuel Dexter Parkhurst,** son of Daniel D. Parkhurst (75) and Sarah Lamb, born December 7th, 1847, at Springfield, Pa.; married, March 24th, 1875, Ida M. Stratford, who was born at Rochelle, Ill., May 7th, 1852. His business is that of a traveling salesman, and he resides at Waukegan, Ill. They had three children:

85 OLIVER LELAND, born January 31st, 1876; died August 7th, 1876.

86 FRANK DEXTER, born March 1st, 1878.

87 HAROLD McLEAN, born August 11th, 1893.

---

76 **Beeby Boyd Parkhurst,** son of Josiah Parkhurst (49) and Rachel Harkness, born February 8th, 1824, at Springfield, Pa.; married, August 21st, 1848, Emeline Mack, at Addison, Steuben County, N. Y. They reside at Waukegan, Ill. They had four children:

88 IDA A., born October 15th, 1849; married, January 12th, 1871, J. A. Woodworth.

89 EVA M., born June 4th, 1852; married, October 18th, 1881, John R. Lawrence.

90 FRANK, born September 10th, 1856; died April 13th, 1859.

91 NORA A., born September 12th, 1862; died January 12th, 1878.

---

88 **Ida A. Woodworth,** daughter of Beeby B. Parkhurst (76) and Emeline Mack, born October 15th, 1849, at Addison, N. Y.; married, January 12th, 1871, James A. Woodworth, at Rochelle, Ill. They reside at Corinne, Utah. They had six children:

92 LULA MAY, born February 22d, 1872, at Rochelle, Ill.

93 JAMES BEEBY, born March 5th, 1874, at Highland Park, Ill.

94 NEWTON BOOTH, born February 25th, 1876; died September 5th, 1880, at Cortland, Ill.

95 FRANK LUCIUS, born March 25th, 1878; died April 8th, 1890, at Highland Park, Ill.

96   IDA PEARL, born April 27th, 1880, at Cortland, Ill.
97   VIRGINIA, born October 5th, 1888, at Highland Park, Ill.

----

89   **Eva M. Lawrence,** daughter of Beeby B. Parkhurst
(76) and Emeline Mack, born June 4th, 1852, at Addison, N.
Y.; married, October 18th, 1881, John R. Lawrence, at Cortland, Ill.; now resides at Waukegan, Ill. They had two
children :
98   NELLIE EVALINE, born September 25th, 1882, at
Mechanicsville, Ia.
99   JOHN ABBOTT, born May 29th, 1886, at Highland Park,
Ill.; died November 1st, 1886.

----

77   **Cordelia Chandler,** daughter of Josiah Parkhurst (49)
and Rachel Harkness, born January 17th, 1827, at Springfield, Pa.; married, November 2d, 1845, Horace Chandler, at
Sullivan, Tioga County, Pa. He was born December 19th,
1819, in Susquehanna County, Pa.; died at Gurnee, Ill.,
November 19th, 1878. She died October 5th, 1885, at
Gurnee, Ill. They had two children :
100   FELICIA JANE, born May 27th, 1847, at Warren, Ill.;
died November, 1847.
101   ELLA LOUISE, born June 30th, 1850; married, December, 18th, 1867, Henry Shepard.

----

101   **Ella Louise Shepard,** daughter of Horace Chandler
and Cordelia Parkhurst (77), born June 30th, 1850, at Warren,
Ill.; married, December 18th, 1867, Henry Shepard. They
reside at Waukegan, Ill., having a summer home at Gurnee,
Ill. They had one child :
102   LOLA ADELINE, born March 7th, 1878.

50 **Sarah Maria Evans,** daughter of John Parkhurst
(37) and Sarah Bullard, born April 10th, 1793, at Marlborough,
N. H.; married, September 5th, 1813, William Evans. They
came with her father to Springfield, Pa., in the fall of 1813.
The two-story frame house, that was built about 1817, is still
standing (1897). She was a favorite daughter, had the same
keen blue eyes, sweet disposition, and was a gentle and
patient mother. She died August 21st, 1837, at Elkland, Pa.,
and a few years later her body was removed to the cemetery
at Addison, N. Y. William Evans died February 16th, 1846,
at Lawrenceville, Pa. They had nine children, all born at
Springfield, Pa. :

103 ELIZA ANN, born November 17th, 1816; died January
18th, 1818.

104 SARAH MARIA, born September 16th, 1818; married,
August 24th, 1842, Dr. Reuben P. Brown.

105 ALLISON H., born May 4th, 1821; married (1st), May,
1846, Abigail Haven; (2d) July 6th, 1849, Laura Haven.

106 HARRY BALDWIN, born November 18th, 1823; died
May 30th, 1825.

107 JOHN PARKHURST, born June 11th, 1826; died September, 1826.

108 MARTHA ROSETTA, born June 5th, 1827; married,
September 5th, 1849, Thomas J. Lake.

109 MARY E., born September 27th, 1830; died December
9th, 1830.

110 WILLIAM MICAJAH, born December 21st, 1831; married, December 6th, 1860, Harriet McNair.

111 CURTIS PARKHURST, born November 3d, 1834; married, April 17th, 1856, Lydia A. Bennett.

104 **Sarah Maria Brown,** daughter of William Evans
and Sarah Maria Parkhurst (50), born September 16th, 1818,
at Springfield, Pa.; married, August 24th, 1842, Dr. Reuben
P. Brown. He was born April 1st, 1818, at Springfield, Pa.
At the age of eighteen he began the study of medicine, and
graduated from Hobart Medical College, Geneva, N. Y. In

1849 he settled at Addison, N. Y., where he practiced medicine continuously for forty years, to the time of his death, which occurred September 15th, 1885. He was one of the most successful physicians in that section of the state. Always as ready to visit the poor as the rich, his loss to the community was deeply felt. He was survived seven years by his wife, who died at Addison, July 30th, 1892. They had three children, two born at Springfield, Pa., and Gertrude M., born at Addison, N. Y. :

112   SARAH H., born December 22d, 1843; died in 1848.

113   RUSH P., born December 14th, 1847; married June 2d, 1869, Georgie N. Cowley.

114   GERTRUDE M., born November 14th, 1851; married, October, 1870, A. H. Erwin.

---

113   **Dr. Rush P. Brown,** son of Dr. Reuben P. Brown and Sarah Maria Evans (104), born December 14th, 1847, at Springfield, Pa. He graduated at New York University Medical College in 1873. He was associated with his father several years prior to his death. On June 2d, 1869, he married Georgie N. Cowley, daughter of Calvin Cowley and Mary Millard, who was born at Lawrenceville, Pa., February 10th, 1849. They reside at Addison, N. Y. They had one child :

115   MILLARD R., born July 24th, 1870; resides at Addison.

---

114   **Gertrude M. Erwin,** daughter of Dr. Reuben P. Brown and Sarah Maria Evans (104), born November 14th, 1851, at Addison, N. Y.; married, October, 1870, Arthur H. Erwin. She died December 28th, 1889, at her home in Addison. They had two children :

116   AGNES M., born July 23d, 1871; married, June 15th, 1892, Allen M. Munroe.

117   FRANCES G., born September 4th, 1872; married, May 18th, 1892, V. Willard Tyler.

116 **Agnes M. Munroe,** daughter of A. H. Erwin and Gertrude M. Brown (114), born July 23d, 1871, at Addison, N. Y.; married, June 15th, 1892, Allen M. Munroe, of Buffalo, N. Y.

117 **Frances G. Tyler,** daughter of A. H. Erwin and Gertrude M. Brown (114), born September 4th, 1872, at Addison, N. Y.; married, May 18th, 1892, V. Willard Tyler, of Buffalo, N. Y.

105 **Allison H. Evans,** son of William Evans and Sarah Maria Parkhurst (50), born May 4th, 1821, at Springfield, Pa.; married (1st), May, 1846, Abigail Haven. She died April 23d, 1848, leaving a babe five weeks old. Married (2d), July 6th, 1849, Laura M. Haven. She died November 19th, 1882, at Lawrenceville, Pa. He died March 16th, 1881, at Lawrenceville, Pa. He had one child by his first wife and five children by his second wife:

118 ALLENA M., born March 17th, 1848; married (1st), May 4th, 1873, James M. Harrison; (2d) October 6th, 1894, Marcus T. Nye.

119 ALTON C., born March 9th, 1852; married, April 22d, 1875, Phebe D. Lugg.

120 FRANK E., born January 27th, 1854; married (1st), April 12th, 1881, Ida M. Hazlett; (2d) January 7th, 1891, Jessie Swift.

121 HATTIE R., born December 4th, 1862; married, January 24th, 1883, G. E. Haven.

122 NETTIE L., born September 9th, 1866; married, November 3d, 1884, Dr. M. R. Pritchard.

NELLIE H., born June 21st, 1868; died July 27th, 1872.

118 **Allena M. Harrison,** daughter of Allison H. Evans (105) and Abigail Haven, born March 17th, 1848, at Lawrenceville, Pa.; married (1st), May 4th, 1873, James M.

Harrison; (2d) October 6th, 1894, Marcus T. Nye. She had four children by her first husband:

123   HATTIE L., born February 5th, 1875, at Deerfield, Pa.; died November 16th, 1880.

124   STELLA M., born October 4th, 1876; married, August 10th, 1895, William E. Nye.

125   ROYAL WESLEY, born February 27th, 1885, at Lawrenceville, Pa.

126   JAMES H., born June 25th, 1886, at Elmer, Pa.; died June 28th, 1886.

---

119   **Alton C. Evans,** son of Allison H. Evans (105) and Laura M. Haven, born March 9th, 1852, at Lawrenceville, Pa.; married, April 22d, 1875, at Nelson, Pa., Phebe D. Lugg, daughter of Robert S. and Rebecca Lugg. He is a farmer and resides at Lindley, N. Y. They had two children, born at Lawrenceville, Pa. :

127   LEAH R., born March 27th, 1876.

128   DOLLIE, born June 18th, 1887.

---

120   **Frank E. Evans,** son of Allison H. Evans (105) and Laura M. Haven, born January 27th, 1854, at Lawrenceville, Pa.; married (1st), April 12th, 1881, Ida M. Hazlett. She died March 9th, 1884. Married (2d), January 7th, 1891, Jessie Swift. She died December 22d, 1894. He is a farmer and resides at Nelson, Pa. He had two children, Vera M., by his first wife, and Norma Bell, by his second wife :

129   VERA M., died January 12th, 1886, aged two years and eleven months.

130   NORMA BELL, born October 7th, 1894.

---

121   **Hattie R. Haven,** daughter of Allison H. Evans (105) and Laura M. Haven, born December 4th, 1862, at Lawrenceville, Pa.; married, January 24th, 1883, G. E. Haven. They reside in Elmira, N. Y.

122 **Nettie L. Pritchard,** daughter of Allison H. Evans (105) and Laura M. Haven, born September 9th, 1866, at Lawrenceville, Pa.; married, November 3d, 1884, Dr. M. R. Pritchard. They reside at Harrison Valley, Pa. They had four children:

131 OTTO L., born June 24th, 1886; died March 28th, 1887.

132 VERA, born April 24th, 1888; died November 5th, 1889.

133 FLORENCE, born November 27th, 1890.

134 GLENN EVAN, born February 20th, 1894.

---

108 **Martha Rosetta Lake,** daughter of William Evans and Sarah Maria Parkhurst (50), born June 5th, 1827, at Springfield, Pa.; married, September 5th, 1849, Thomas J. Lake. He was a merchant a few years. His life was occupied in teaching, a calling he was very successful in. He was an ordained minister of the Methodist Episcopal church; was postmaster at Athens, Ala., for five years; served in the civil war two years. They reside at Bartow, Fla. They had seven children:

135 WILTON HAMILTON, born October 5th, 1850, at Hartford, Pa.; married, August 29th, 1893, Annie M. Anderson.

136 SELWYN, born February 22d, 1852, at Elkland, Pa.; died October 20th, 1868.

137 LUCIA MARIA, born April 24th, 1854, at Elkland, Pa.; married, November 4th, 1873, Edgar E. Webster.

138 CLARA E., born July 11th, 1856, at Addison, N. Y.; died May 18th, 1857.

139 ELBERT S., born February 4th, 1863, at Austin, Minn.; resides at Bartow, Fla.

140 ARTHUR EDWARD, born February 11th, 1867, at Austin, Minn.; died October 1st, 1867.

141 EDWARD NELSON, born June 13th, 1869, at Austin, Minn.; resides in Chicago, Ill. He is an electrician and civil engineer.

135　**Wilton Hamilton Lake,** son of Thomas J. Lake and Martha R. Evans (108), born October 5th, 1850, at Hartford, Pa.; married, August 29th, 1893, Annie M. Anderson, daughter of Henry VanVoorhis and Rachel Demorest, born in New York City, N. Y., October 9th, 1855. He is a carpenter and resides at Bartow, Fla.

137　**Lucia Maria Webster,** daughter of Thomas J. Lake and Martha R. Evans (108), born April 24th, 1854, at Elkland, Pa.; married, November 4th, 1873, Edgar E. Webster, son of Levi Webster and Mary P. Smith. He served twenty-one months in the army. His present business is lumbering. He owns and operates a steam saw mill near Bartow, Fla. They had seven children :

142　CLARA MABEL, born August 24th, 1874.

143　ARTHUR LAKE, born October 22d, 1877.

144　HERBERT WARREN, born July 8th, 1880.

145　EDGAR E., born May 16th, 1882.

146　LUCIA BELLE, born March 23d, 1888.

147　L. SELWYN, born September 18th, 1892.

148　BENJAMIN HARRISON, born July 19th, 1895.

110　**William Micajah Evans,** son of William Evans and Sarah Maria Parkhurst (50), born December 21st, 1831, at Springfield, Pa.; married, December 6th, 1860, Harriet H. McNair, daughter of Hugh McNair and Mary Fowler, born in Livingston County, N. Y., December 2d, 1833, and died at Amherst, Va., October 23d, 1881. He now lives at Amherst, Va. They had three children :

149　OTTO LOUIS, born November 12th, 1861, at Lyons, Ia.; married, December 8th, 1891, Mary Randolph.

150　MARY FOWLER, born May 21st, 1865, at Elmira, N. Y.; married, March 15th, 1892, William Dillard.

151　WILLIAM HUGH, born July 8th, 1875, at Castile, N. Y.

149 **Otto Louis Evans,** son of William Micajah Evans
(110) and Harriet H. McNair, born November 12th, 1861,
at Lyons, Ia.; married, December 8th, 1891, Mary Randolph,
daughter of Peyton Randolph and Mary E. Fisher, born in
Greenbrier County, W. Va., August 21st, 1870. They had
two children:

152 PEYTON RANDOLPH, born October 18th, 1892.

153 HARRIET McNAIR, born September 10th, 1894.

150 **Mary Fowler Dillard,** daughter of William Micajah
Evans (110) and Harriet H. McNair, born May 21st, 1865,
at Elmira, N. Y.; married, March 15th, 1892, Judge William
Dillard, son of General Jerisha Washington Dillard, born in
Amherst County, Va., August 23d, 1846. They had one
child:

154 WILLIAM EVANS, born February 11th, 1893.

111 **Curtis Parkhurst Evans,** son of William Evans
and Sarah Maria Parkhurst (50), born at Springfield, Pa.,
November 3d, 1834; married, April 17th, 1856, Lydia A.
Bennett, daughter of John W. Bennett and Elizabeth Shoff,
born December 18th, 1834, in New Hampshire. They now
reside at Elkland, Pa. His business is that of a carpenter
and builder. They had three children:

155 ELIZABETH S., born March 12th, 1857; married, May
24th, 1882, Franklin B. Orser.

156 BERTHA H., born August 28th, 1865; married, December 24th, 1890, Charles E. Smith.

157 CURTIS P., Jr., born October 25th, 1877. He resides
at Elkland, Pa.

155 **Elizabeth S. Orser,** daughter of Curtis Parkhurst
Evans (111) and Lydia A. Bennett, born March 12th, 1857,
at Elkland, Pa.; married, May 24th, 1882, Franklin B. Orser.
They had one child:

158 MARION O., born January 15th, 1890.

51   **Dr. Curtis Parkhurst,** son of John Parkhurst (37) and Sarah Bullard, was born July 2d, 1794, at Marlborough, N. H. At the age of sixteen he began to teach school, studying in the meantime to prepare himself for college. He graduated from Dartmouth Medical College at Hanover, N. H., in 1819. He settled at Lawrenceville, Pa., and at once began the practice of his profession. After ten years of active work, ill health compelled him to retire from general practice.

In 1828-9 he represented the counties of Lycoming, Potter, McKean and Tioga, in the Legislature. In 1829-30 Bradford and Tioga Counties formed a district, and he was their representative. In 1840 he was elected sheriff of Tioga County, and served from 1841 until 1844.

On the 15th day of March, 1847, Francis P. Shenk, Governor of Pennsylvania, appointed him to be the Associate Judge of the Court of Common Pleas of Tioga County for five years. He was largely instrumental in the building of the Tioga railroad, from Corning, N. Y., to Blossburg, Pa., as an outlet for the Blossburg coal mines, in which Ex-Governor Horatio Seymour, of Deerfield, N. Y., and others, were interested as co-partners.

While sheriff he lived at Wellsboro, and while there the first Presbyterian meeting in that village was held in the court house, his wife (our mother) ringing the court house bell for the service. Soon after a Presbyterian church was established there, in which he took a great interest. He often lectured, and was a ready speaker and debater. A sturdy Democrat in politics, he kept himself well informed on all topics of the day. He was a quiet and retiring man in manner, and a life-long member of the Presbyterian church.

On November 11th, 1830, he married Jane Ann Kasson, of Syracuse, N. Y. She was born at North Adams, Mass., April 5th, 1811, the daughter of Ambrose Kasson and Laura Hall. Her parents moved to Syracuse about 1816, and later to Deerfield, N. Y. Her grandfather was Calvin Hall, of Chester, Mass., who was born in 1760. He served twice in the Revolution: at Fort Ann, on Lake Champlain, in 1777, in Colonel

John Brown's regiment, and in the same regiment in 1780, where he was engaged in the battle of Stone Arabia, N. Y., October 19th, 1780, in which the colonel and forty of his regiment were killed.

Curtis Parkhurst died at the homestead in Lawrenceville, Pa., on June 5th, 1872. He was survived fifteen years by his wife, who died at Lawrenceville, October 20th, 1887. Theirs was no easy task, in a new country, to faithfully rear a large family. That they conscientiously fulfilled their trust is amply evidenced by the traditions of sixty years, and gratefully acknowledged by their descendants. They had eight children :

159   KASSON, born March 12th, 1832 ; married, September 11th, 1855, Harriet Mills.

160   SEELY, born April 2d, 1834 ; died August 13th, 1836.

161   HELEN, born February 17th, 1837 ; married, November 5th, 1859, Gabriel T. Harrower.

162   ELIZA FORD, born February 8th, 1840 ; married, January 1st, 1861, Wilbur W. Fish.

163   JOHN FOSTER, born February 17th, 1843 ; married, July 22d, 1886, Alice McMaster.

164   JAY CURTIS, born June 26th, 1845 ; married, May 3d, 1870, Caroline Williams.

165   CATHERINE SEELY, born May 18th, 1847 ; married, February 15th, 1883, Hugh McFadden.

166   GABRIEL HARROWER, born February 14th, 1849 ; married, September 9th, 1891, Lillian O. Holloway.

159   **Kasson Parkhurst,** son of Curtis Parkhurst (51) and Jane Ann Kasson, born March 12th, 1832, at Lawrenceville, Pa. ; married (1st), September 11th, 1855, Harriet Mills, daughter of Rev. Sidney and Laura Mills. She died March 23d, 1858, leaving a baby boy six months old. Married (2d), January 2d, 1861, Mary Kinsey. She died August 6th, 1885. There were no children by the second marriage. He studied law with Judge John Ryan, was admitted to practice when twenty-two years of age. His early death, June 3d, 1863, cut

short a professional career that promised to win honors. He had one child by his first marriage :

167   EDWIN KASSON, born September 2d, 1857 ; died August 14th, 1880.

161   **Helen Parkhurst Harrower,** daughter of Curtis Parkhurst (51) and Jane Ann Kasson, born February 17th, 1837, at Lawrenceville, Pa. ; married, November 5th, 1859, Col. Gabriel T. Harrower. He was born September 25th, 1816, at Guilford, Chenango County, N. Y. In his childhood he moved to Lindley, N. Y., where the greater part of his life was spent, largely engaged in lumbering and farming. In 1852 he was elected sheriff of Steuben County, and in 1862 was active in raising the 161st Regiment of New York Infantry, of which he was commissioned the colonel. He was assigned to the department of the Gulf. He was brevetted Brigadier-General for gallant and meritorious service in the field. In 1871 he was elected to the state senate, where he served two years. He was a communicant in the Presbyterian church. He died August 15th, 1895, at Lawrenceville, Pa. He had four children by this marriage :

168   DAVID CURTIS, born September 9th, 1862 ; resides at Wilkes-Barre, Pa., and is a lawyer.

169   CATHERINE, born September 17th, 1860 ; resides at Lawrenceville, Pa.

170   FRANK PARKHURST, born September 5th, 1865 ; married, February 18th, 1890, Kate E. Jones.

171   ANTOINETTE, born October 31st, 1868 ; resides at Lawrenceville, Pa.

170   **Frank Parkhurst Harrower,** son of Gabriel T. Harrower and Helen Parkhurst (161), born September 5th, 1865, at Lawrenceville, Pa.; married, February 18th, 1890, Kate E. Jones, daughter of Edgar Jones and Sarah M. Esty. She was born October 26th, 1868, at Fall Brook, Pa. They reside at Wilkes-Barre, Pa., where he has charge of the collection department in his brother's law office. They had one child :

172   CURTIS GABRIEL, born August 16th, 1894.

Jane A. Parkhurst.

162 **Eliza Parkhurst Fish,** daughter of Curtis Parkhurst (51) and Jane Ann Kasson, born February 8th, 1840, at Lawrenceville, Pa.; married, January 1st, 1861, Wilbur Wheeler Fish, son of Joseph Fish and Lucia Field, born August 9th, 1834, at Tioga, Pa. In 1859 he started in the mercantile business at Great Valley, N. Y. In 1862 he went to East Saginaw, Mich., where he carried on a large wholesale and retail store until 1872, when he retired from business temporarily, but in 1878 located in Elmira, N. Y., continuing the dry-goods business until 1892, when he retired. He started for a trip around the world with his family in 1892. After reaching Japan, Mrs. Fish's ill health necessitated the abandonment of the trip. They returned home with their son, Edwin C., the elder son, Wilbur P., continuing. The first three children were born at Saginaw, Mich., and Edwin Cook at Lawrenceville, Pa. They had four children :

173 Son, born March 13th, 1868; died March 30th, 1868.

174 WILBUR PARKHURST, born February 22d, 1869; married, September 4th, 1894, Susan D. Church.

175 FOSTER PARKHURST, born February 15th, 1872; died May 5th, 1872.

176 EDWIN COOK, born February 20th, 1876; resides at Elmira, N. Y. He is an organist and teacher of music.

174 **Wilbur Parkhurst Fish,** son of Wilbur Wheeler Fish and Eliza Ford Parkhurst (162), born February 22d, 1869, at East Saginaw, Mich.; married, September 4th, 1894, Susan Dudley Church, daughter of Edwin L. Church and Augusta Bull, born at Bath, N. Y., December 5th, 1872. He graduated at Yale College in 1892, and made the trip around the world in 1892-3. He studied law in the office of John F. Parkhurst, his uncle, and was admitted to the bar in 1895. He is now practicing law in Bath, N. Y. He was appointed United States Loan Commissioner for Steuben County by Governor Black in 1897.

163   **John Foster Parkhurst,** son of Curtis Parkhurst
(51) and Jane Ann Kasson, born February 17th, 1843, at
Wellsboro, Pa. He received his education at Lawrenceville,
Pa. At the age of twenty he moved to Bath, N. Y., and
began the study of law in the office of Judge Guy H. Mc-
Master. Two years later he was admitted to the bar, and at
once began the practice of his profession. In 1872 he formed
a partnership with Judge McMaster, which lasted until the
death of the latter in 1887. The firm enjoyed a large and
important practice in both state and federal courts, John F.
devoting his especial attention for many years to bankruptcy
and equity cases in the United States courts. Among the
important cases successfully carried through the state courts
by him was that of Griffith Jones against the Bradford Oil
Company, in which, after seven years of litigation and three
jury trials, the client recovered three hundred acres of oil land,
valued at several hundred thousand dollars, by virtue of a tax
title which cost him less than fifty cents an acre. Another
important case was that of Silvey against Lindsey, in which
the Court of Appeals passed upon the constitutional right of
the thousand or more inmates of the New York State Soldiers'
and Sailors' Home to acquire a voting residence in the town
of Bath. In 1891 he was associate counsel for the Republican
senators in the famous mandamus cases.

He has been always an earnest and active Republican.
Since 1889 he has been chairman of the Republican committee of Steuben County, and since 1890 has represented
the Twenty-ninth Congressional District, comprising the
counties of Steuben, Chemung, Schuyler and Seneca, in the
Republican State committee, of whose executive committee
he is also a member. He was delegate to the Republican
National Conventions of 1888, 1892 and 1896. He has edited
The Steuben Courier since 1890; is a stockholder and vice-
president of the Farmers' and Mechanics' Bank, of Bath, and
vice-president of the Bath and Hammondsport Railroad Company. He was delegate-at-large to the New York State Constitutional Convention in 1894, in which he served as a

member of the judiciary and suffrage committees, and as
chairman of the committee on county, town and village
officers.   He is also a member of the Empire State Society of
the Sons of the American Revolution, and an elder and trustee
in the Presbyterian church.   He is a member of the Masonic
fraternity.   He has traveled extensively in Europe.   On one
of his trips abroad he visited the place called " Parkhurst,"
on the Isle of Wight, where our ancestors many centuries ago
made their home.   He is now a Judge of the State Court of
Claims, having been appointed by Governor Black in 1897
for a term of six years.   He heard and decided as referee the
great litigations between the Mutual Life Insurance Company,
of New York, and David C. Robinson, of Elmira, N. Y.,
involving a million and a half dollars.

On July 22d, 1886, he married Alice McMaster, daughter
of Guy H. McMaster and Amanda Church, who was born in
Bath, N. Y., October 30th, 1860.   They had two children :

177   JULIET, born June 29th, 1887 ; died December 4th, 1888.
178   GUY McMASTER, born September 26th, 1889.

164   **Jay Curtis Parkhurst**, son of Curtis Parkhurst (51)
and Jane Ann Kasson, born June 26th, 1845, at Lawrenceville, Pa. ; married (1st), May 3d, 1870, at East Saginaw, Mich.,
Caroline Williams, daughter of Ellery G. Williams and
Caroline Lyon, born September 15th, 1846, at Canandaigua,
N. Y.   She died May 14th, 1888, at Lawrenceville, Pa.   Married (2d), June 29th, 1893, at Philadelphia, Pa., Goertner E.
Mumford, daughter of the late Sylvester and Teresa Mumford,
of Waynesville, Ga.   In 1862 he went to East Saginaw, Mich.,
with his brother-in-law, W. W. Fish.   Ten years later he engaged in business for himself, but poor health soon compelled

him to abandon active business. He returned to Lawrenceville, where he has resided for the past twenty years. He is
an elder in the Presbyterian church. His two sons reside in
Bath—John Foster, 2d, confidential clerk to General Wm. F.
Rogers, at the New York State Soldiers' and Sailors' Home,
and Fred W., official stenographer of the Surrogate's court
and for his uncle, John F. Parkhurst. He had six children
by his first wife, of which the first three were born at Saginaw,
Mich., and the last three at Lawrenceville, Pa. :

179   BESSIE B., born July 10th, 1871 ; died October 14th, 1873.

180   JOHN FOSTER, 2d, born August 26th, 1873 ; resides at
Bath, N. Y.

181   FREDERICK WILLIAMS, born August 14th, 1875 ;
resides at Bath, N. Y.

182   JAMES B., born June 14th, 1878 ; died June 17th, 1878.

183   ISABEL W., born September 17th, 1880 ; died August
25th, 1881.

184   KATHARINE M., born September 3d, 1883.

165   **Catherine Parkhurst McFadden,** daughter of
Curtis Parkhurst (51) and Jane Ann Kasson, born May 18th,
1847, at Lawrenceville, Pa. ; married, February 15th, 1883,
Hugh McFadden, son of Benjamin McFadden and Martha E.
Harper. He was born December 23d, 1846, at Sterling,
Cayuga County, N. Y. His early life was spent on the farm.
He attended the Falley Seminary at Fulton, N. Y., three
years. In March, 1868, he went to DeKalb County, Ill. In
1875 he engaged in the wholesale cigar and tobacco business
at Bloomington, Ill., which he continued for eight years. In
1884 he removed to Danville, Ill., engaging in the drug
business. In August, 1891, he removed to Chicago, Ill.,

Lillian Parkhurst

where he opened a loan and collection office. He is a lawyer by profession, admitted to the Cook County bar June 12th, 1895. They reside at 6838 Sherman street, Chicago, Ill. They had three children, the first, Joel P., was born at Lawrenceville, Pa., and the others at Danville, Ill. :

185   JOEL PARKHURST, born December 5th, 1883.

186   BENJAMIN CURTIS, born March 17th, 1885.

187   EDWIN COOK, born October 3d, 1887.

---

166   **Gabriel Darrower Parkhurst,** son of Curtis Parkhurst (51) and Jane Ann Kasson, born February 14th, 1849, at Lawrenceville, Pa.; married, September 9th, 1891, at Fort Worth, Texas, Lillian O. Holloway, daughter of Jesse R. Holloway and Laura Canady, who was born at Georgetown, Ill., October 19th, 1868. They had one child, a son, born August 20th, 1896, and died the same day. The mother died two days later, and was buried at Lawrenceville, Pa. She was a woman of true Christian character, with a bright, sunny disposition, which won her many friends and made her beloved by all who knew her.

In 1883 he entered into partnership with N. J. Thompson and opened the first strictly jobbing house for hats and caps in Elmira, N. Y. After five years he sold his interest to his partner and went to El Dorado, Kan., where he, with others, organized the Merchants' National Bank, of which he was elected vice-president, and was actively engaged in the management of the bank until January, 1896, when he resigned and retired from active business. He is now a partner in the El Dorado Mining Company, at Robinson, Colo., and is a member of the Empire State Society of the Sons of the American Revolution. He now resides at Bath, N. Y.

52   **Dr. Dexter Parkhurst,** son of John Parkhurst (37) and Sarah Bullard, born September 21st, 1797, at Marlborough, N. H.; married, July 4th, 1823, Marian Speer. She was born August 27th, 1801. He located at Mansfield, Tioga County, Pa., where he had an extensive practice for many years. In 1836 he moved to Mainsburg, Pa., on his farm, where he devoted a great deal of time and money to the growing of choice fruits. He was an expert with his rifle, and many are the stories told of his skill with it. He resembled his father in appearance—had the same beautiful white hair, keen eyes, and quiet manner. How well the writer remembers his visit to our home during Kasson's last sickness. He thought him the handsomest old gentleman that he had ever seen. He died June 2d, 1866, at the homestead in Mainsburg. He was survived four years by his wife, who died at Mainsburg, October 14th, 1870. They had six children, the first four being born at Mansfield:

188   PORTER DEXTER, born March 15th, 1824; married (1st), June 5th, 1849, Sarah D. Pinkham; (2d) September 24th, 1860, Sarah Ophelia Young.

189   DR. PHILANDER J., born August 5th, 1827; died September 17th, 1851.

190   DR. PHILEMON, born August 19th, 1830; married, January 1st, 1852, Rosilla Fox.

191   BALDWIN, born March 8th, 1832; married, January 3d, 1856, Celia E. Maine.

192   SARAH MARIA, born June 29th, 1837; married, February 3d, 1857, Edwin R. Maine.

193   CHARLES FRANK, born November 14th, 1849; married, December 5th, 1872, Jennie C. Cudworth.

188   **Porter Dexter Parkhurst,** son of Dexter Parkhurst (52) and Marian Speer, born March 15th, 1824, at Mansfield, Pa.; married (1st), June 5th, 1849, Sarah D. Pinkham. She

died at Mainsburg, Pa., May 8th, 1859. Married (2d), September 24th, 1860, Sarah Ophelia Young, daughter of Francis and Belle Young, who was born at Covington, Pa., March 28th, 1837, and died at Painted Post, N. Y., September 18th, 1883. He was for many years a merchant at Painted Post; now resides at Lestershire, N. Y. He had four children by his second wife:

194   FRANK DEXTER, born September 29th, 1861; married, February 26th, 1888, Katharine E. Cheney.

195   MARK C., born May 26th, 1863; died July 18th, 1882.

196   MARIA BELLE, born June 11th, 1867; married, July 27th, 1892, George Bullis.

197   CHARLES LESLIE, born February 23d, 1871; married, June 26th, 1895, Luella L. Aldrich.

---

194   **Frank Dexter Parkhurst,** son of Porter Dexter Parkhurst (188) and Sarah Ophelia Young, born September 29th, 1861, at Covington, Pa.; married, February 26th, 1888, Katharine E. Cheney, daughter of Hugh L. Cheney and Mary E. Mook. She was born at Groveport, Ohio, June 13th, 1865. They reside at Columbus, Ohio. They had one child:

198   MARY FLORENCE, born July 27th, 1890.

---

196   **Maria Belle Bullis,** daughter of Porter Dexter Parkhurst (188) and Sarah Ophelia Young, born June 11th, 1867, at Covington, Pa.; married, July 27th, 1892, George Bullis. They reside at Lestershire, N. Y. They had one child:

199   MILTON P., born May 24th, 1893.

---

197   **Charles Leslie Parkhurst,** son of Porter Dexter Parkhurst (188) and Sarah Ophelia Young, born February 23d, 1871, at Painted Post, N. Y.; married, June 26th, 1895, Luella Louise Aldrich, daughter of Alphonso J. Aldrich and Mary Beach. She was born December 1st, 1871, at Nunda, N. Y. He is a stenographer, and they reside at Buffalo, N. Y.

190   **Dr. Philemon Parkhurst,** son of Dexter Parkhurst
(52) and Marian Speer, born August 19th, 1830, at Mansfield,
Pa.; married, January 1st, 1852, Rosilla Fox, daughter of
John Fox and Deborah Rickard. She was born at Mainsburg, Pa., November 3d, 1833. He died at Scipio, N. Y.,
July 27th, 1893. He was a successful practitioner, and took
great interest in the Methodist church, of which he was a
member. In politics he was a Republican. His widow resides at Scipio, N. Y. They had four children :

200   EUGENE FOX, born March 2d, 1853; married, December 15th, 1874, Tella Strong.

201   EDGAR DEXTER, born October 31st, 1855; married,
October 25th, 1876, Grace M. Simons.

202   EMMA TILLIE, born August 12th, 1861; married, October 19th, 1881, Lloyd Howell.

203   JOHN RAYMOND, born December 3d, 1873; resides at
Scipio, N. Y.

---

200   **Eugene Fox Parkhurst,** son of Philemon Parkhurst
(190) and Rosilla Fox, born March 2d, 1853, at Mainsburg,
Pa.; married, December 15th, 1874, Tella Strong, daughter
of John Strong and Theodocia Lucas, of Mainsburg, Pa. He
died November 13th, 1896. His home was at Spring Valley,
Fillmore County, Minn. They had two children :

204   FRED EUGENE, born December 15th, 1877.

205   LELA ROSILLA, born November 28th, 1885.

---

201   **Edgar Dexter Parkhurst,** son of Philemon Parkhurst (190) and Rosilla Fox, born October 31st, 1855, at Mainsburg, Pa.; married, October 25th, 1876, Grace Marian Simons,
daughter of Jeremiah Simons and Caroline Bishop, who was
born October 1st, 1857, at Union Springs, N. Y. They reside at Scipio, N. Y. They had four children :

206   SEWARD, born December 11th, 1879.

207   BLANCHE, born October 11th, 1883; died March 30th, 1893.

208   EDITH, born January 12th, 1896.

209   HELEN, born September 15th, 1892.

202 **Emma Tillie Howell,** daughter of Philemon Parkhurst (190) and Rosilla Fox, born August 12th, 1861, at Mainsburg, Pa.; married, October 19th, 1881, Lloyd Howell, son of Isaac Howell and Johanna Beardsley. He was born April 19th, 1858, at Scipio, N. Y. They reside at Owasco Lake, N. Y. They had one child:

210 HAROLD C., born May 25th, 1888.

191 **Baldwin Parkhurst,** son of Dexter Parkhurst (52) and Marian Speer, born March 8th, 1832, at Mansfield, Pa.; married, January 3d, 1856, Celia E. Maine, daughter of Horace S. Maine and Minerva B. Beecher. She was born July 23d, 1836, at Mainsburg, Pa., and died November 9th, 1890. He died January 27th, 1888. He was an active merchant at Mainsburg for many years, and was largely instrumental in the building of the handsome brick Methodist church. They had no children.

192 **Sarah Maria Maine,** daughter of Dexter Parkhurst (52) and Marian Speer, born June 29th, 1837, at Mainsburg, Pa.; married, February 3d, 1857, Edwin R. Maine, son of John Maine and Nancy Spencer. He was born February 28th, 1830, at Mainsburg, Pa. She died August 14th, 1866. They had two children:

211 HOWARD P., born January 23d, 1858; married, December 13th, 1883, Mary E. Elliott.

212 CHARLES L., born February 17th, 1865; married, October 11th, 1893, Jennie E. Herrington.

211 **Howard Park Maine,** son of Edwin R. Maine and Sarah Maria Parkhurst (192), born at Mainsburg, Pa., January 23d, 1858; married, December 13th, 1883, Mary E. Elliott, daughter of Orson V. Elliott and Celia Kelly. She was born at West Covington, Pa., April 25th, 1861, and died at Mans-

field, Pa., February 19th, 1894. He now resides at Mainsburg. They had five children.

213   JOSEPH HOWARD, born April 28th, 1885.

214   EDWIN ELLIOTT, born June 19th, 1887.

215   MALCOLM, born September 3d, 1892; died August 26th, 1893.

216 *Twins.* { CHARLES ALBERT, born February 6th, 1894.

217   { HOWARD ALBA, born February 6th, 1894; died December 15th, 1894. •

---

212 **Dr. Charles L. Maine,** son of Edwin R. Maine and Sarah Maria Parkhurst (192), born February 17th, 1865, at Mainsburg, Pa.; married, October 11th, 1893, Jennie E. Herrington, daughter of Charles Herrington and Sarah J. Mathers, who was born at Wellsboro, Pa., January 30th, 1868. He graduated May 15th, 1892, at the College of Physicians and Surgeons, Baltimore, Md. He settled at Helvetia, Pa., and at once began the practice of his profession. In 1893 he was elected a member of the board of visiting physicians of Adrian Hospital, at DeLancey, Pa. In 1894 he was appointed railroad surgeon of the M. V. R. R.

---

193 **Charles Frank Parkhurst,** son of Dexter Parkhurst (52) and Marian Speer, born November 14th, 1849, at Mainsburg, Pa.; married, December 5th, 1872, Jennie Cudworth, daughter of James Cudworth and Lydia J. Whittaker. She was born in Richmond Township, Tioga County, Pa., October 7th, 1853. They reside on the farm at Mainsburg, Pa. They had one child :

218   CARL LEON, born March 27th, 1876; married, February 18th, 1895, Nettie L. Perry.

---

218 **Carl Leon Parkhurst,** son of Charles F. Parkhurst (193) and Jennie Cudworth, born March 27th, 1876, at Mainsburg, Pa.; married, February 18th, 1895, Nettie L. Perry, daughter of Almeron M. Perry and Jennie Davey, born March 25th, 1877, at Richmond, Pa. They reside at Mainsburg, Pa.

53 **Joel Parkhurst,** son of John Parkhurst (37) and Sarah
Bullard, born April 8th, 1800, at Marlborough, N. H.; married (1st), November 16th, 1835, Emeline R. Allen, daughter of
Edward Allen and Anna Richard, born December 13th, 1815,
at Bridgewater, N. Y. She died at Elkland, Pa., October 29th,
1854. Married (2d), May 14th, 1856, Widow Martha H. Steel,
daughter of Benjamin Harrower and Dinah Mersereau, who
was born at Lawrenceville, Pa., June 27th, 1822, and died in
New York City, February 11th, 1889, and was buried at
Elkland, Pa. At the age of seventeen years he commenced
teaching school. This was continued until he was twenty-
two years old, his spare time being devoted to the study of
medicine. In the spring of 1822 he went to Michigan as a
government surveyor. Later he returned to Richmond, N. H.,
and went to work as a clerk for two years at $150 per year
and board. On settling with his employer he received his
salary in merchandise, and went to Mansfield, Pa., where he
started in business for himself. In 1826 he went to Lawrenceville, Pa., and formed a co-partnership with his brother, Curtis,
which was continued until 1828. He then went to Elkland,
Pa., and his business soon grew to large proportions, which
made him the leading merchant of the valley. He continued
extending his business until the Rebellion, when he was able
to take the county bonds, issued by the commissioners of
Tioga County, and furnished the means for the payment of
bounties to our volunteers. About this time he opened a
bank, taking into the company his son-in-law, Charles L.
Pattison, and John Parkhurst, under the name of Joel Parkhurst & Co. He was largely instrumental in the building of
the Cowanesque Valley railroad, of which he was made
president. In 1876 he erected the present brick High School
building and gave it to the village. He also gave the Presbyterian church its parsonage. He was an elder in the church,
and was identified with its interests, contributing liberally
toward the support of the gospel. Politically he was a Republican, and one of the most influential citizens of the county.
He died at Elkland, Pa., December 6th, 1884, leaving an

estate valued at more than a million dollars. In 1890 his
children erected a beautiful memorial church in his memory,
at a cost of twenty thousand dollars, at Elkland, Pa.

He had eight children by his first wife, Emeline R. Allen,
and two children by his second wife, Martha Harrower :

219   EDWARD JOEL, born October 14th, 1837 ; died August
15th, 1840.

220   JOHN CLAY, born December 25th, 1839 ; died March
13th, 1850.

221   SARAH MARIA, born November 9th, 1841 ; died June
18th, 1850.

222   ANNA STELLA, born November 30th, 1843 ; married,
October 21st, 1868, Charles L. Pattison.

223   MARY, born March 1st, 1846 ; died March 4th, 1846.

224   FRANK, born January 24th, 1848 ; died April 26th, 1860.

225   CURTIS S., born March 10th, 1852 ; died March 13th,
1852.

226   CHARLES, born August 10th, 1854 ; died December 6th,
1854.

227   SUSAN AMELIA, born May 26th, 1857 ; married, March
9th, 1887, J. B. Grier.

228   BENJAMIN H., born October 28th, 1861 ; married, October 7th, 1896, Marian M. Moon.

---

222   **Anna Parkhurst Pattison,** daughter of Joel Park-
hurst (53) and Emeline R. Allen, born November 30th, 1843, at
Elkland, Pa. ; married, October 21st, 1868, Charles L. Pattison, son of Thurman Pattison and Susan Wilson Bishop. He
was born February 16th, 1841, at Chester, Warren County,
N. Y. The family moved to Lawrenceville, Pa., in 1847.
He went to Fall Brook, Pa., in the employ of the Fall Brook
Coal Company, in 1860, and soon rose to the position of
cashier of the company. In 1869 he removed to Elkland,
Pa., and became a partner in the banking firm of Joel Park-
hurst & Co., a business in which he showed great ability. In

1882 he organized the company which built the Addison and Northern Pennsylvania railroad, he becoming its president. His business became so extensive that he took up the study of law, for the service it could be to him in managing his large estate. In 1888 he was admitted to the Tioga County bar. On August 1st, 1889, the name of the bank was changed to C. L. Pattison & Co., which was continued until his death, in Philadelphia, Pa., April 10th, 1896. Mr. Pattison was a liberal minded man, both in theory and practice. He was of high moral character and rare business ability. He gave freely from his large means, but without ostentation, many of his charitable gifts being unknown, except to the beneficiaries themselves. They had no children.

227 **Susan Parkhurst Grier,** daughter of Joel Parkhurst (53) and Martha Harrower, born at Elkland, Pa., May 26th, 1857; married, March 9th, 1887, Rev. J. B. Grier. As a child at school she was remarkable for her extraordinary insight and rare common sense. She was a beautiful, noble woman. She died at Geneva, Switzerland, September 25th, 1891, and is buried at Elkland, Pa. Her husband, John Boyd Grier, was born at Danville, Pa., August 26th, 1843. He was graduated at Lafayette College in 1864. He was a private in the 138th Pennsylvania regiment in 1863, and was principal of the Wellsboro Academy in 1864–1865. He studied theology at Alleghany in 1867–1869, and was adjunct professor of modern languages and rhetoric at Lafayette and author of studies in the English of Bunyan in 1869–1872. Since 1873 he has been pastor at Lawrenceville, Pa., Jacksonville, Fla., Danville and Lewisburg, Pa. He was Commencement Orator at Lafayette College in 1889, at which time the degree of D. D. was conferred upon him by his Alma Mater. Since the death of his wife he has resided at Elkland, Pa. They had no children.

228   **Benjamin Harrower Parkhurst,** son of Joel Park-
hurst (53) and Martha Harrower, born at Elkland, Pa.,
October 28th, 1861 ; married, October 7th, 1896, Marian
Murray Moon, youngest daughter of Rev. Solomon H. Moon,
D. D., Ph. D., and Charlotte Brandt. In 1882 he was urged
to take the presidency of the Addison and Northern Pennsylvania railroad, but declined, accepting a place as director.
He has always been actively interested in religious work.
When quite young he united with the Presbyterian church
at Elkland, of which he is an elder and trustee, and superin-
tendent of the Sunday school. He has had charge of the
choir for the past fifteen years, is a fine singer and a cultured
student of music. His business interests have been very extensive, adding much to the prosperity of his native village.
He has traveled extensively in this country and Europe. He
resides at Elkland, Pa.

54   **Martha Parkhurst Seelye,** daughter of John Parkhurst (37) and Sarah Bullard, born April 2d, 1803, at Marlborough, N. H. ; married, July 25th, 1827, Micajah Seelye.
. She died at Lawrenceville, Pa., February 1st, 1856. He was
the first white child born in the town of Lindley, Steuben
County, N. Y. He was an active business man all his life,
and his lumber interests were extensive. He died at Lawrenceville, Pa., October 27th, 1864. They had three children :

229   LINDSLEY PARKHURST, born August 20th, 1828 ;
married, December 30th, 1853, Martha Booth.

230   SARAH EVANS, born December 31st, 1834 ; resides in
Toledo, Ohio. She is a fine singer and a highly cultured
musician.

231   ELIZABETH, born August 11th, 1837 ; died November
9th, 1855.

229   Lindsley Parkhurst Seelye, son of Micajah Seelye
and Martha Parkhurst (54), born August 20th, 1828; married,
December 30th, 1852, at Ballston Spa, N. Y., Martha Booth,
daughter of Selbues Booth, and Lucretia Foot, born May
20th, 1830, at Ballston Spa. He was a merchant at that place
for many years, and his widow still resides there. He died
June 10th, 1868. They had two children :

232   CAROLINE KENT, born October 20th, 1853; married,
September 6th, 1876, William H. Burr.

233   SARAH ELIZABETH, born December 26th, 1854; married, October 22d, 1884, William M. VerPlank.

---

232   Caroline Kent Burr, daughter of Lindsley Parkhurst
Seelye (229) and Martha Booth, born October 20th, 1853, at
Ballston Spa, N. Y.; married, September 6th, 1876, William
Hulbert Burr. She died in New York City, May 1st, 1894.
They had three children :

234   MARIAN ELIZABETH, born June 29th, 1881.

235   WILLIAM FAIRFIELD, born February 7th, 1884.

236   GEORGE LINDSLEY, born August 29th, 1889.

---

233   Sarah Elizabeth VerPlank, daughter of Lindsley
Parkhurst Seelye (229) and Martha Booth, born December
26th, 1854, at Ballston Spa, N. Y.; married, October 22d,
1884, William M. VerPlank. They had no children.

---

55   Ebenezer Fisk Parkhurst, son of John Parkhurst
(37) and Sarah Bullard, born November 1st, 1807, at Marlborough, N. H.; married, November 8th, 1829, Demis Brown,
daughter of Aden Brown and Lydia Parmenter, born July
24th, 1809, in Massachusetts, and died at Springfield, Pa.,
on February 9th, 1887. He was only six years of age when
his father moved from New Hampshire, and his entire life
was spent on the farm. He was a Christian gentleman, and

took an active part in all church matters. He died at the
old home, October 15th, 1892. They had five children :

237   LYDIA, born March 1st, 1832 ; married, October 5th, 1853,
Frank Loveland.

238   JOHN C., born August 21st, 1833 ; married, July 4th,
1864, Frankie Smith.

239   CYNTHIA H., born March 2d, 1836 ; died February 18th,
1842.

240   ELSIA A., born February 11th, 1841 ; married, January
30th, 1861, Rodney H. Cooley.

241   NORTHWAY, born December 2d, 1844 ; married, June
18th, 1884, Mary E. King.

237   **Lydia Loveland,** daughter of Ebenezer F. Parkhurst
(55) and Demis Brown, born March 1st, 1832, at Springfield,
Pa. ; married, October 5th, 1853, Frank Loveland. She died
at Elkland, Pa., February 16th, 1886. They had one child :

242   FRANK P., born February 7th, 1857 ; died April 26th,
1865.

238   **John C. Parkhurst,** son of Ebenezer F. Parkhurst
(55) and Demis Brown, born August 21st, 1833, at Springfield, Pa. ; married, July 4th, 1864, Frankie Smith, daughter
of Seth Smith and Harietta Huggins. He died at Springfield,
Pa., March 2d, 1865. They had no children.

240   **Elsia A. Cooley,** daughter of Ebenezer F. Parkhurst
(55) and Demis Brown, born February 11th, 1841 ; married,
January 30th, 1861, Rodney H. Cooley, of Troy, Pa. She
died February 3d, 1885, at Troy, Pa. They had two children :

243   ANNA P., born December 11th, 1869 ; married, April
27th, 1892, Albion Budd.

244   HELEN, born March 26th, 1863 ; died May 19th, 1863.

. 243　**Anna Parkhurst Budd**, daughter of Rodney H. Cooley and Elsia A. Parkhurst (240), born December 11th, 1869, at Troy, Pa. ; married, April 27th, 1892, Albion Budd. They reside at Troy, Pa.

241　**Northway Parkhurst,** son of Ebenezer F. Parkhurst (55) and Demis Brown, born December 2d, 1844, at Springfield, Pa. ; married, June 18th, 1884, Mary E. King, daughter of Samuel King and Margaret A. Pine, of Lansingburg, N. Y. He died at the old homestead at Springfield, Pa., October 29th, 1896, and his widow still resides there. They had two children :

245　ETTIE, born June 18th, 1886 ; died July 21st, 1886.

246　GERTRUDE M., born September 13th, 1890.

www.ingramcontent.com/pod-product-compliance
Lightning Source LLC
Chambersburg PA
CBHW030853260626
47169CB00008B/2515